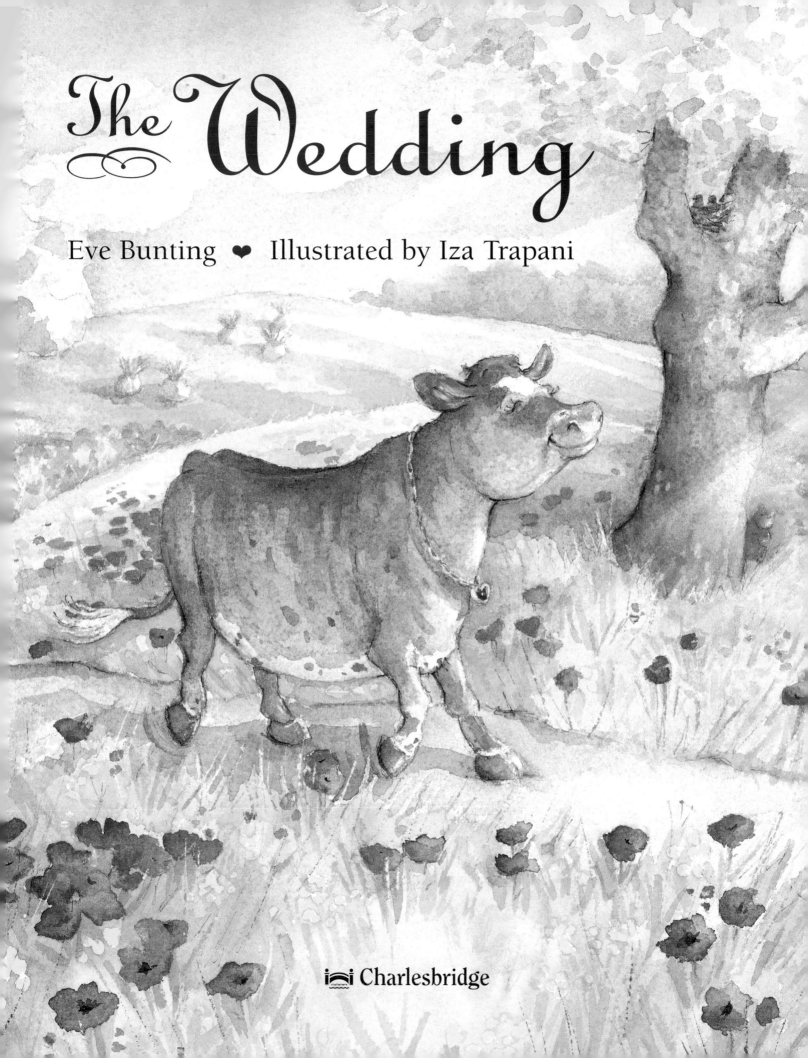

The Wedding

Eve Bunting ❤ Illustrated by Iza Trapani

ini Charlesbridge

To my friend and scribe, Susan Rubin
— E. B.

To Kim, Danny, Rachelle, Joshua, and Maxx with love
— I. T.

First paperback edition 2005
Text copyright © 2003 by Eve Bunting
Illustrations copyright © 2003 by Iza Trapani

Published by Charlesbridge
85 Main Street
Watertown, MA 02472
(617) 926-0329
www.charlesbridge.com

Library of Congress Cataloging-in-Publication Data
Bunting, Eve, 1928–
The wedding / Eve Bunting ; illustrated by Iza Trapani.
p. cm.
Summary: One by one, Miss Brindle Cow encounters a group of animals
who are late for a wedding and agrees to carry them there.
ISBN-13: 978-1-58089-040-3; ISBN-10: 1-58089-040-7 (reinforced for library use)
ISBN-13: 978-1-58089-118-9; ISBN-10: 1-58089-118-7 (softcover)
[1. Weddings—Fiction. 2. Brides—Fiction. 3. Cows—Fiction.
4. Animals—Fiction. 5. Stories in rhyme.] I. Trapani, Iza, ill. II. Title.
PZ8.3.B92   We 2003
[E]—dc21   2002010449

Manufactured in China
(hc) 10 9 8 7 6 5 4 3
(sc) 10 9 8 7 6 5 4 3 2 1

Illustrations done in watercolor on Arches 300 lb. cold press watercolor paper
Display type and text type set in Cathedral and Berkeley
Color separations, printing & binding by P. Chan & Edward, Inc.
Production supervision by Brian G. Walker
Designed by Diane M. Earley

Miss Brindle Cow, all sweetly brown,
walked along the path to town,
listening to the wedding bells—
the wedding bells of Saint Michelle.

She saw a pig beneath a tree.
"Alas!" Pig cried. "I've cranked my knee!
I'm the organist in church.
I'll have to leave them in the lurch.
This wedding won't be quite as good!
I'd play my heart out if I could."

Miss Brindle Cow said, "Don't despair!
Climb on my back. I'll take you there."

They spied a turtle, lying down.
He said, "I'm on my way to town.
I wish I wasn't quite so slow.
I started out a week ago.

"I'm the florist, Pomeroy,
and weddings are my special joy.
I won't be there, I'm sad to say.
There'll be no flowers in church today."

Miss Brindle Cow said, "Don't be gloomy.
Climb on Pig's back. It's nice and roomy."

A duck sat, rubbing her sore feet.
"I'm made to swim and quack and eat.
Walking's very hard for me,
so this is a catastrophe.

"I'm the pastor. Who'll be there
to hear the vows and say a prayer?"

Miss Brindle Cow said, "Please calm down.
I will take you into town."

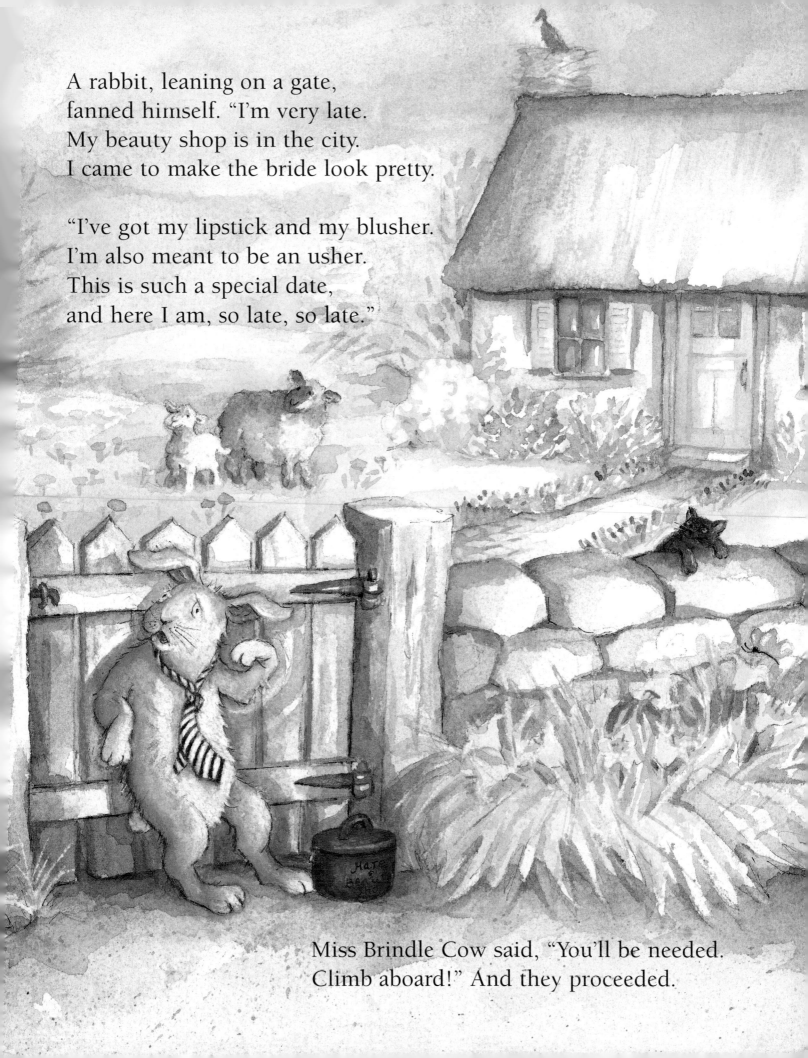

A rabbit, leaning on a gate,
fanned himself. "I'm very late.
My beauty shop is in the city.
I came to make the bride look pretty.

"I've got my lipstick and my blusher.
I'm also meant to be an usher.
This is such a special date,
and here I am, so late, so late."

Miss Brindle Cow said, "You'll be needed.
Climb aboard!" And they proceeded.

A chipmunk that the turtle knew
said, "I don't know what to do.
I'm the chef for this affair,
and I've been wandering who knows where.
I'm all worn out. I'm quite exhausted.
At least the wedding cake is frosted!

"But still I have to make the hash—
the corn, the meal, the hot maize mash.
There'll be no wedding banquet food—
and they expect a multitude."

"Climb on," Miss Cow said. "Don't be shy.
I hope you won't mind sitting high."

A small brown thrush flew overhead.
"I'm off to Saint Michelle's," he said.
"They asked if I would fly along
and sing a sacred wedding song.

" 'O Promise Me' is very nice.
So nice I think I'll sing it twice.
I'd really like to come with you
if that's an okay thing to do?"

Miss Brindle Cow came to a stop.
"We'd love it! Perch up there on top."

They sweetly sang "O Promise Me,"
their voices blending tenderly.
They sang of love, all starry-eyed,
and then they sang "Here Comes the Bride."

Thrush said, "I see the church! We're here!
Miss Brindle Cow, you were so dear!
I hope we weren't too much for you!"
"Oh no," Cow said. "I'm good as new.

"I am woman. I am strong.
I'm happy that you came along."

Duck bowed. "Please join us all inside."

"Yes," Brindle Cow said. . . .

"I'm the bride."